SNOW-MAN
IT'S A GAS!

By Tommy Donbavand
& Steve Beckett

TITLES IN THE SNOW-MAN SET

HOT HOT HOT!
WINDY POPS!
STONE AGE
IT'S A GAS!
WHAT A DRIP!
COLD FRONT

Badger Publishing Limited
Oldmedow Road,
Hardwick Industrial Estate,
King's Lynn PE30 4JJ

Telephone: 01438 791037
www.badgerlearning.co.uk

2 4 6 8 10 9 7 5 3 1

It's a Gas!
ISBN 978-1-78464-355-3

Publisher: Susan Ross
Senior Editor: Danny Pearson
Editorial Coordinator: Claire Morgan
Illustration: Steve Beckett
Designer: Fiona Grant

IT'S A GAS!

CONTENTS

Cole Day lives in the town of Shiverton with his parents, his sister, Winter, and pet dog, Jeff.

All a bit boring until, one day... *COSSSSHHH!* A stray snowball hit Cole on the back of his head!

But it wasn't just any snowball. It was a RADIOACTIVE snowball! And it turned Cole into Snow-Man – the world's chilliest superhero!

Now, whenever he munches on a raw carrot, Cole's body transforms into a big, white, fluffy man of action!

It's down to Snow-Man and his team, **THIN ICE** and **FROSTBITE**, to defeat the world's nastiest weather-changing villains.

Bad guys, you'd better freeze! SNOW-MAN is slip-sliding your way...

CAST OF CHARACTERS

Cole

Winter

Jeff

SNOW-MAN

Misty Morning

VOCABULARY

disappeared	separated
mysterious	embarrass
dungarees	trickster

Chapter One

Wispy

Cole Day hurried down the garden to the shed. He pulled open the door, jumped inside and quickly closed it behind him, cutting off the only source of light.

"Wow!" he said to himself. "It's really dark in here!"

"I know!" said a voice that made Cole jump.

"Who's that?" asked Cole.

"Who do you think it is?" hissed the other person. "It's me, Winter, your sister!"

"Oh," said Cole. "Sorry. I couldn't tell."

"You couldn't tell it's me by the sound of my voice?" said Winter.

"It might have been Dad."

"No," said Winter. "Dad's voice is a lot deeper than mine."

"Yes," said a deep voice from the back of the dark shed. "Much deeper."

"What are you doing in here, Dad?" asked Cole.

Dad thought for a second. "It's my shed."

"That's true," said Winter. "But you don't normally come and hide down here."

"Who said I'm hiding?" said Dad. "I might have been looking for something."

"Were you looking for something?" asked Cole.

"Yes," said Dad. "I was looking for a good hiding place."

"What are you hiding from?" asked Cole.

"Not what," said Winter. "Who. We're all in here hiding from Mum."

"And the new recipe idea she's had for lunch," added Dad.

"Sounds horrible, doesn't it?" said Cole.

"**WOOF!**" barked a doggy voice.

"Jeff?" said Cole, Winter and Dad together.

"**COO-EE!**" shouted Mum from outside in the garden.

Everyone in the shed fell silent.

"Where is everyone?" called Mum.

She was standing in the doorway, holding a tray of different sized and different coloured balls.

"You all disappeared before you could try my new recipe!"

Chapter Two

Thin

In the shed, Cole, Dad, Winter and Jeff stayed quiet.

"It's got a theme this time," said Mum. "There are melon balls, meatballs, cheese balls, golf balls dipped in gravy, a tennis ball filled with custard! Oh, and there's something round and hard that I found behind the fridge that I think started out life as a sprout."

In the shed, Cole, Dad, Winter and Jeff stayed VERY quiet.

They heard Mum's mobile ring, and her voice as she answered the call.

"Hello? Yes, I noticed it was getting a bit foggy. A special weather report from the Town Hall? I'll be right there. I'll even bring a snack for everyone! Goodbye."

Dad waited until the sound of Mum's footsteps had disappeared. "I think she's gone," he said.

"Then let's get out of the shed," said Cole. "I can't see a thing in here…"

He pushed the door open and all four of them stepped outside.

"I can't see much out here, either," said Winter.

Dad waved a hand in front of his face, but he couldn't see it. "This must be the fog Mum had to go and give an urgent weather report about," he said.

"It's the thickest fog ever," said Cole.

"We have to be careful not to get separated," said Winter. "Everyone hold hands, and we'll head back to the house together."

"**BARK!**" said Jeff.

So, in a line, the Day family inched their way up the garden.

They had almost reached the back door when they realised they weren't alone.

"Who's there?" demanded Winter.

But the new arrival just laughed crazily...

"*PAH-HA-HA-HA-HA-HA-HAH!*"

...and then there was a rustle of material.

Cole, Winter and Dad shuffled up the steps and into the kitchen.

Now out of the fog, they could see each other clearly again – and it was quite a strange sight.

Both Cole and Dad had their trousers down around their ankles.

Chapter Three
Thick

"Who did that to us?" cried Dad.

"And why did they leave you alone?" Cole asked Winter.

Winter tugged at the shoulder straps of her outfit. "Dungarees," she explained. "These weren't going anywhere!"

"**WOOF!**" said Jeff standing in front of Mr Day.

Everyone followed the pooch's gaze.

"Dad…" said Cole. "Why do you have yellow pixies all over your underwear?"

Dad's cheeks flushed red. "I, er… thou… I mean… there was… and they…" he gabbled.

Then he quickly pulled up his trousers and raced upstairs.

"Who would do something like this, and why?" asked Winter.

Cole pulled up his own trousers, fishing a raw carrot from his pocket as he did so. "Let's find out..."

He took a bite from the carrot.

Instantly, a frozen whirlwind blew up around the kitchen and wrapped itself around the trio.
Icicles flashed, rain showered and snow settled at their feet.

A moment later – exactly where Cole had been – stood a white giant of a figure, dressed in a top hat and red scarf.

He had eyes as black as coal, and what remained of the carrot formed his nose.

This was SNOW-MAN – the world's chilliest superhero!

Standing beside Snow-Man were the two members of his super-team – a young girl named Thin Ice, and a brave-looking dog called Frostbite.

"First of all," said Snow-Man, "we need a name for this trouser trickster. Everyone, put on your Snow-Goggles!"

Thin Ice produced three pairs of goggles with glowing lenses and handed them out.

Then Snow-Man and his team stepped outdoors.

"PAH-HA-HA-HA-HA-HA-HAH!"

"Hey! This way!" said Snow-Man.

Although the fog was still as thick as ever, the powerful goggles allowed the three heroes to see clearly around them.

As they ran, they passed men, women and children who were all busy pulling their trousers back up.

Chapter Four

Dense

"I still don't get it," said Thin Ice. "Why pull people's trousers down?"

"To embarrass them, of course," explained Snow-Man.

"Well, yes…" said Thin Ice. "But, with this thick fog all around, no one can see you've had your trousers pulled down."

Snow-Man skidded to a halt. "That is a very good point," he said.

"*WOOF! BARK! BARK! SNUFFLE!*" suggested Frostbite.

"Good thinking, boy!" cried Snow-Man. "What if these poor people aren't the intended victims? What if these trouser tuggings are just a practice run?"

"Then who is the real target?" said Thin Ice.

"*PAH-HA-HA-HA-HA-HA-HAH!*"

"Let's go right to the source for that!" said Snow-Man, pointing across the street. "There's our culprit – Misty Morning!"

On the opposite side of the road stood a young girl in a bright green superhero suit and cape.

She wore shorts over her tights, and thick, padded boots.

"You can see me?" gasped Misty Morning.

"Thanks to these goggles, as plain as the carrot on my face!" said Snow-Man. "Long time no see, Misty!"

"Wait," said Thin Ice. "You know her?"

Snow-Man nodded. "Thin Ice, Frostbite – meet Misty Morning. Shiverton's original superhero!"

Thin Ice stared at Snow-Man. "What?"

"It's true," said Misty Morning, crossing the street. "I was the good guy in those days. I could stop any villain by smothering their crime scenes with fog. The police always arrived before the bad guys could find their way out of my mysterious mist!"

"So, what happened?" asked Thin Ice.

Misty Morning sighed. "I was at the Town Hall, being given an award by the mayor. I spotted a thief in the crowd and filled the street with fog – but it was a trap! The real bad guys used my mist as a cover, and they stole the mayor's pet dog!"

"*GRRRRR!*" said Frostbite, hiding behind Snow-Man's leg.

"The mayor blamed me for what happened, and I lost my job as the town's superhero. But, today I'll get my revenge!"

And, with that, Misty Morning spun on the spot to whirl up another blanket of fog.

Then she vanished.

Chapter Five

Solid

"It's the mayor!" said Snow-Man. "He's the target! She wants to pull down his trousers and make him look ridiculous!"

"On live TV," said Thin Ice. "Mum's broadcasting her special weather report from the Town Hall, and the mayor would never miss the chance to join in!"

"Let's go!"

The trio reached the Town Hall just as the weather report went live on air.

Despite the dense fog, a large crowd of people had gathered to watch – and many of them had already had their trousers pulled down.

"PAH-HA-HA-HA-HA-HA-HAH!"

With his goggles, Snow-Man could see Misty Morning creeping closer and closer to the mayor.

He could also see the tray of round food – untouched, sitting beside the cameraman.

That gave him an idea.

"You know, it's not just Mum's food that comes in balls!" cried Snow-Man. "I do, too!"

Scooping a hand into his own stomach, Snow-Man pulled out a perfectly round lump of snow and took aim.

He would only get one shot at this.

Just as Misty Morning grabbed the mayor's belt, he launched his snowball.

COOOSSSHHH!

The snowball caught Misty Morning on her left ear, sending her crashing to the ground.

CRASH!

Her concentration lapsed, and the fog began to lift.

Immediately, the mayor's two bodyguards spotted the threat and pounced, arresting the former superhero.

"Another case closed!" beamed Snow-Man.

"But it's left me with a bit of a hole in my stomach."

"We can fill that," smiled Thin Ice. "What do you want to eat?"

"Is Mum cooking?"

"*GRRRR!*" said Frostbite, shaking his head.

Snow-Man laughed. "Then I haven't the foggiest idea!"

QUESTIONS

1. Where did everyone hide from Mum? *(page 6)*

2. What had Mum filled a tennis ball with? *(page 9)*

3. What are the lenses in the Snow-Goggles like? *(page 15)*

4. Who was pulling down trousers all over town? *(page 18)*

5. Who was the main target? *(page 22)*

6. What did Snow-Man throw at Misty? *(page 24)*

MEET THE
AUTHOR AND ILLUSTRATOR

THE AUTHOR

Tommy Donbavand spent his
school days writing stories
in which more popular kids
than him were attacked
and devoured by slavering
monsters. Years later, he's still
doing the same thing – only now
people pay him for it. The fools!

THE ILLUSTRATOR

Steve Beckett has a robot arm
that is programmed to draw
funny pictures. He likes
playing with toy soldiers
and dreams of being an ace
survival expert. He is scared
of heights, creepy crawlies and
doesn't like camping!